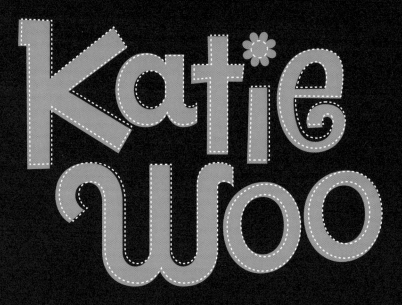

Katie Woo

Katie and the Haunted Museum

by Fran Manushkin

illustrated by Tammie Lyon

PICTURE WINDOW BOOKS
a capstone imprint

Katie Woo is published by Picture Window Books,
A Capstone Imprint
1710 Roe Crest Drive
North Mankato, Minnesota 56003
www.mycapstone.com

Library of Congress Cataloging-in-Publication Data
Names: Manushkin, Fran, author. | Lyon, Tammie, illustrator. |
  Manushkin, Fran. Katie Woo.
Title: Katie and the haunted museum / by Fran Manushkin ; illustrated
  by Tammie Lyon.
Description: North Mankato, Minnesota : Picture Window Books, [2019] |
  Series: Katie Woo | Summary: Katie, her father, JoJo, and Pedro are
  on a special sleepover at the museum; but at night the dark halls
  are spooky, and it is easy to imagine that the dinosaurs are ghosts
  haunting the museum—and when Mr. Woo disappears the children
  become frightened.
Identifiers: LCCN 2018038090| ISBN 9781515838432 (hardcover) |
  ISBN 9781515840480 (pbk.) | ISBN 9781515838463 (ebook pdf)
Subjects: LCSH: Woo, Katie (Fictitious character)—Juvenile fiction. |
  Chinese Americans—Juvenile fiction. | Natural history museums—
  Juvenile fiction. | Dinosaurs—Juvenile fiction. | Fear—Juvenile fiction. |
  CYAC: Chinese Americans—Fiction. | Museums—Fiction. | Sleepovers—
  Fiction. | Dinosaurs—Fiction. | Fear—Fiction.
Classification: LCC PZ7.M3195 Kak 2019 | DDC 813.54 [E] dc23
LC record available at https://lccn.loc.gov/2018038090

Graphic Designer: Bobbie Nuytten

Printed and bound in the United States of America.
PA49

Table of Contents

Chapter 1
Museum Sleepover 5

Chapter 2
More to Explore! 12

Chapter 3
Feeling Frightened 18

Chapter 1
Museum Sleepover

Katie asked JoJo, "Are you ready to spend the night at the museum?"

"I'm not sure," said JoJo. "I've never slept next to dinosaurs before."

"My dad says we will
learn a lot," Katie told JoJo.
"Don't forget to pack your
pj's, your sleeping bag, and
your flashlight."

"Wow!" said Katie when

she saw the museum. "There

are cots in every room.

Where should we sleep?"

"Wherever you want,"

said her dad.

"Let's sleep with the sharks," said Pedro.

"No way!" JoJo shivered. "They might give me nightmares."

"I want to sleep with the grizzly bears," said Katie.

"*GRRRR!*" she roared.

"Oooh," joked her dad. "You scared me."

"I can't wait to see the live animals," said Katie.

They saw an eagle and an alligator.

"Wow!" said Katie. "They are very alive."

On the way back to their
cots, Katie waved to the
owls.

"*Hoo, hoo!*" she hooted.

"Stop!" said JoJo. "You
sound like a ghost."

Chapter 2

More to Explore!

The friends' cots were cozy,

and they soon fell asleep.

Suddenly Pedro woke up.

"Yikes!" he yelled. "Something

is pinching my toe!"

Was it an alligator?

No! It was Katie.

"I can't sleep," she said.

"Dad says it's okay to walk
around some more."

JoJo jumped up. "Don't
leave me alone with the
bears."

Katie turned on her

flashlight and led the way.

They saw big and small

elephants walking in a line.

"Let's do that too," said

Katie.

"Cool!" Her dad smiled.

In the moose room, Pedro said, "Let's be moose too!"

Katie and JoJo and Pedro ran down halls, making loud moose calls.

"Moooo! Mooo! Moooooo!"

JoJo joked, "We sound like cows!"

"Stop!" yelled JoJo. "I lost one of my slippers. We have to go back and find it."

"Don't worry," said Katie.

"My dad knows the way."

"Where is he?" asked

Pedro.

They looked around.

He was gone!

Chapter 3
Feeling Frightened

JoJo grabbed Katie's hand, saying, "We'd better run. That dinosaur is staring at us."

"No way," said Katie. "He's been dead for millions of years."

"Yikes!" yelled Pedro, pointing at a shadow. "That animal is *not* dead!

"Right," said Katie. "*Now* we should run!"

They ran, but the animal
came closer and closer and
closer!

"Wait!" said Katie,

turning around. "I know

that animal. It's my dad."

She hugged him, saying,

"Your long ears were

JoJo's bunny

slipper."

JoJo told Katie's dad,
"Thank you for finding my
slipper."

"I'm so glad I did," said
Katie's dad. "But finding all
of you was the best."

Pedro said, "I'm glad this
place isn't haunted."

"Me too," said JoJo.

"These grizzlies look like big
teddy bears!"

"They do," said Katie.

"Good night, grizzlies," whispered Katie.

"Sleep tight, grizzlies," said Pedro.

"Good night, teddy bears," said JoJo.

And they slept very well.

About the Author

Fran Manushkin is the author of many popular picture books, including *Happy in Our Skin; Baby, Come Out!; Latkes and Applesauce: A Hanukkah Story; The Tushy Book; Big Girl Panties; Big Boy Underpants;* and *Bamboo for Me, Bamboo for You!* There is a real Katie Woo—she's Fran's great-niece—but she never gets in half the trouble of the Katie Woo in the books. Fran writes on her beloved Mac computer in New York City, without the help of her two naughty cats, Chaim and Goldy.

About the Illustrator

Tammie Lyon began her love for drawing at a young age while sitting at the kitchen table with her dad. She continued her love of art and eventually attended the Columbus College of Art and Design, where she earned a bachelor's degree in fine art. After a brief career as a professional ballet dancer, she decided to devote herself full time to illustration. Today she lives with her husband, Lee, in Cincinnati, Ohio. Her dogs, Gus and Dudley, keep her company as she works in her studio.

Glossary

flashlight (FLASH-lite)—a light that can be carried around and is powered by a battery

grizzly bear (GRIZ-lee BAIR)—a large, brown bear that lives in western North America

haunted (HAWN-ted)—visited by a ghost

museum (myoo-ZEE-uhm)—a place where interesting objects of art, history, or science are displayed

nightmare (NITE-mair)—a frightening or unpleasant dream

worry (WUR-ee)—to be nervous or anxious about something

Let's Talk

1. Of the areas of the museum mentioned in the story, which area would you want to sleep in? Would you be scared to sleep in any of the areas? Why or why not?

2. Katie and her friends were scared by something that wasn't actually scary at all—the shadow of JoJo's bunny slipper! Has something like this ever happened to you? What happened?

3. The story ends with the children telling the grizzly bears good night. Do you think they slept well after that? Explain your reasoning.

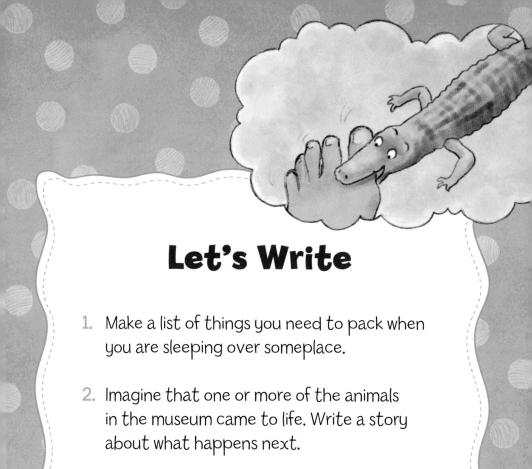

Let's Write

1. Make a list of things you need to pack when you are sleeping over someplace.

2. Imagine that one or more of the animals in the museum came to life. Write a story about what happens next.

3. Pretend you are building a museum. Make a list of at least eight display rooms you will have, then create a map that shows where each room is. Label the rooms.

Having Fun with Katie Woo!

In this Katie Woo book, a spooky shadow scared Katie, JoJo, and Pedro. But not all shadows are scary. This activity shows you how to have lots of fun with shadows!

Draw With Shadows

What you need:

- white paper

- a light source like the sun or a desk lamp

- small plastic figurines—animals work great!

- something to draw with like pens, pencils, markers, or crayons

What you do:

1. Place your paper on a flat surface. If you are working outside and using the sun as your light source, you can even work on the ground!

2. Set a plastic figurine at the edge of the paper. Place it so that it is between the paper and your light source. It should create a shadow on your paper.

3. Adjust the placement of the paper and figurine until the shadow is the size you want on your paper. (If you are working inside with a lamp, you can also adjust the placement of your lamp.) If your shadow is extra big, you can always tape multiple pieces of paper together.

4. Using a drawing utensil, trace around the edge of your shadow. You've made a shadow drawing! Now you can use more crayons or markers to decorate your drawing any way you wish.

Shadows are longest in the early morning and in the late afternoon, so those are good times to try this fun activity outdoors.

THE FUN DOESN'T STOP HERE!

Discover more at www.capstonekids.com

- ♥ Videos & Contests
- ❀ Games & Puzzles
- ♥ Friends & Favorites
- ❀ Authors & Illustrators

Find cool websites and more books like this one at www.facthound.com. Just type in the Book ID: **9781515838432** and you're ready to go!